OLD TURTLE'S BASEBALL STORIES

OTHER YOUNG YEARLING BOOKS YOU WILL ENJOY:

OLD TURTLE'S WINTER GAMES, *Leonard Kessler*
OLD TURTLE'S RIDDLE AND JOKE BOOK, *Leonard Kessler*
OLD TURTLE'S SOCCER TEAM, *Leonard Kessler*
BULLFROG AND GERTRUDE GO CAMPING, *Rosamond Dauer*
BULLFROG GROWS UP, *Rosamond Dauer*
THE ADVENTURES OF MOLE AND TROLL, *Tony Johnston*
HAPPY BIRTHDAY, MOLE AND TROLL, *Tony Johnston*
NIGHT NOISES AND OTHER MOLE AND TROLL STORIES,
Tony Johnston
MOLE AND TROLL TRIM THE TREE, *Tony Johnston*
MONSTERS IN THE OUTFIELD, *Stephen Mooser*

YEARLING BOOKS/YOUNG YEARLINGS/YEARLING CLASSICS are designed especially to entertain and enlighten young people. Patricia Reilly Giff, consultant to this series, received the bachelor's degree from Marymount College. She holds the master's degree in history from St. John's University, and a Professional Diploma in Reading from Hofstra University. She was a teacher and reading consultant for many years, and is the author of numerous books for young readers.

For a complete listing of all Yearling titles,
write to Dell Readers Service,
P.O. Box 1045, South Holland, IL 60473.

OLD TURTLE'S BASEBALL STORIES

Leonard Kessler

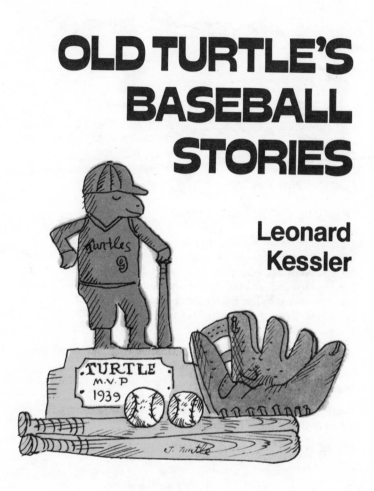

A Young Yearling Book

Published by
Dell Publishing
a division of
Bantam Doubleday Dell Publishing Group, Inc.
666 Fifth Avenue
New York, New York 10103

ISBN: 0-440-40277-8

Reprinted by arrangement with William Morrow & Company, Inc., on behalf of Greenwillow Books

Printed in the United States of America

March 1990

10 9 8 7 6 5 4 3 2

W

To my all-time favorite
baseball players...
"SLATS" MARION, MEL OTT,
SATCHEL PAIGE, JOSH GIBSON,
WILLIE MAYS, THE "BABE,"
TED WILLIAMS, ROGER MARIS,
"HONUS" WAGNER, REGGIE,
ROY FISHMAN,
LENNY ANSELL

OLD TURTLE'S
BASEBALL
STORIES

It was winter.

Cold, cold winter.

Old Turtle sat

by the warm wood stove.

Owl, Frog, Chicken, and Duck

huddled by the stove too.

In the summer

they played baseball.

But in the winter
they told each other...
BASEBALL STORIES.

Old Turtle told
the best stories.
"Tell us a true
baseball story,"
said Frog.

"I saw some of the
greatest players
of all time," said Turtle.
"Who was the greatest pitcher?"
asked Owl.

"The greatest pitcher
was Cleo Octopus,"
Turtle said.

"Great fast ball?"

asked Chicken.

"The fastest," said Turtle.

"Good slow ball?"

asked Duck.

"The slowest," said Turtle.

"Let me tell you

a story about...

CLEO OCTOPUS.

CLEO OCTOPUS
SEA CHAMPS

PITCHER

"It was a very big game.

The score was 0-0,

top of the sixth.

Cleo was the pitcher

for the Sea Champs.

" 'Throw your best pitch.
I'll knock it out
of the park,'
the batter yelled.

"Well, Cleo looked

at the batter a long time.

"Then she threw a...
fast ball,
slow ball,
curve ball,
and knuckle ball.

"All at the same time!
SWISH!

" 'No fair. No fair,'
yelled the fans.
'YOU ARE OUT!'
the umpire shouted."

"The hitter was out?" asked Frog.

"NO," said Turtle.

"Cleo was out.

The umpire tossed her

out of the game.

"Cleo quit baseball.
She did not
want to pitch
just one ball
at a time."

"What did she do then?"

asked Owl.

"She opened a hot dog stand
near the ball park.
She worked there
all by herself.
Greatest hot dog pitcher
that I ever saw,"
said old Turtle.
"Is that a true story?"
asked Duck.
"Every word of it,"
said Turtle.

"Well, who was the
greatest hitter?"
asked Owl.
"Oh, that's easy.
His name was
Melvin Moose,"
said Turtle.

BASEBALL CAR

"Righty or lefty?"
asked Frog.
"Melvin could hit
righty, lefty, and
other ways too!"
Turtle told them.
"What other ways?"
Duck asked.

"Well, let me tell you
a story about...
MELVIN MOOSE.

MELVIN MOOSE
N.Y. MOOSE   1 ST BASE

"It was a big game.

Melvin was at bat.

It was Goose

pitching to Moose.

"Goose threw a wild pitch
right at Melvin's head."
"And what did Melvin do?"
asked Chicken.
"Did he hit the dirt?"
asked Owl.
"Did he duck?" asked Duck.

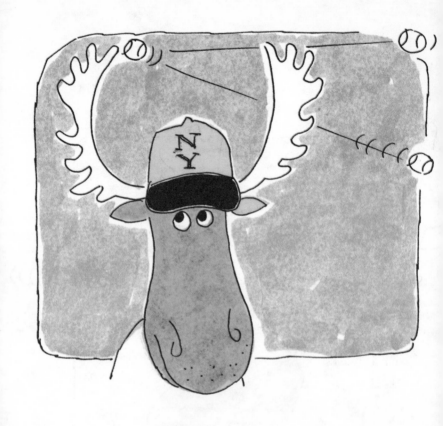

"No," said Turtle.
"Melvin hit that ball
with his antlers.
POW.
It went for a double!"
"Wow," said Frog.

"It was the start
of a new game...
called Mooseball,"
Turtle said.

"Melvin is in the
Mooseball Hall of Fame."

"Is that really true?"
asked Duck.
"Every word of it,"
said Turtle.

"Who was the best
outfielder?" asked Frog.
"Carla Kangaroo,"
said Turtle.
"She played right field,
left field,
and center field."

"All three?" asked Duck.

"At the same time,"
   said Turtle.

"How did she do that?"
   asked Owl.

"Well, let me tell you
a story about...
CARLA KANGAROO.

CARLA KANGAROO
N.J. KANGAROOS
OUTFIELD

"It was a big game.

"The score was

| BLUE SOX | 2 |
| KANGAROOS | 3 |

The bases were full.
'Two outs. Batter up,'
the umpire called
to the Blue Sox.

"The pitcher threw a fast ball.

POW!

The batter hit it.

Back, back it went.

" 'It's going for a home run,'
the Blue Sox shouted.

"Carla hopped and skipped.
She jumped.
But she tripped and
fell down."

"Did she catch the ball?"
asked Owl.
"Did the Kangaroos lose?"
asked Frog.
"Was it a home run?"
asked Chicken.

"NO!" said Turtle.

"NO?" asked Duck.

"Her little baby, Joey,
caught the ball.
The Kangaroos won!"
said Turtle.

"Yeah!" shouted Owl.

"Is this a true story?"
asked Frog.

"Every word of it,"
said Turtle.

"Well, who stole
the most bases?"
asked Chicken.

"Oh, that's my best story,"
Turtle told them.
"It is called . . .

WHO STOLE THE MOST BASES?

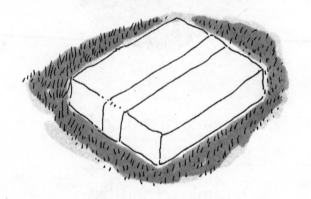

"It was a big game.

The Top Dogs came

to play the Furry Tails.

" 'Who stole first base?'
asked Skunk.
'Who stole second base?'
asked Fox.
'And who stole third base?'
asked Porcupine.

"The bases were gone.

Really gone.

The Top Dogs went

to get new bases.

"That night Skunk and Fox
hid behind the backstop.
'I hear something,' said Skunk.
'I see someone,' said Fox.
'It's the crook,' said Skunk.
'He is stealing our bases.
Let's follow him.'

" 'He is in his house,"

Fox whispered.

They tiptoed inside.

" 'It's RANDY SQUIRREL!'
they shouted.

'We caught you,' said Skunk.
'Why did you
steal our bases?'
he asked.

" 'I want to be
   on your baseball team.
   I am a good base stealer,'
   Randy said.
   'That's not the way
   to steal bases,'
   Skunk told him.
   'We will show you how
   tomorrow,' said Fox.

"Randy was a fast runner.
Skunk showed him
how to steal bases.
He ran.
He slid.

"Soon he was the champ.
When he was on base,
the fans cheered.
'STEAL, RANDY, STEAL!'
they yelled."

"Is that a true story?"
asked Duck.

"Every word of it,"
said Turtle.

"Well, we know
who the greatest
storyteller is,"
said Frog.

"Who?" asked Owl.

"Old TURTLE!"

they all shouted.

LEONARD KESSLER is a popular writer and illustrator of children's books. He is best known for his sports books—*Here Comes the Strikeout*; *Kick, Pass and Run*; *On Your Mark, Get Set, Go*; and *Super Bowl*. He is also the illustrator of *I Was Thinking*, a book of poems by Freya Littledale.

Mr. Kessler was born in Ohio and grew up in Pittsburgh. (His favorite baseball team is the Pirates.) He was graduated from Carnegie Institute of Technology with a degree in Fine Arts, Painting and Design. He lives in New City, Rockland County, New York, where a huge snapping turtle has moved into his swimming pool.